John's WEDDING

Wendy Elmer

authorHOUSE®

AuthorHouse™ LLC
1663 Liberty Drive
Bloomington, IN 47403
www.authorhouse.com
Phone: 1-800-839-8640

Published by AuthorHouse 10/10/2013

ISBN: 978-1-4918-2667-6 (sc)
ISBN: 978-1-4918-2666-9 (e)

CHAPTER 1

May 24th, 2011 was the start of the Memorial Day weekend. The entire police department for the City of Las Vegas was instructed to show up with a smile and a welcoming look on their face. Especially the strip squad. They had to know how to direct people to the different attractions. Even off the strip they had to know about. Most of the time their answer was to take the bus. It got you everywhere.

John Reyes was working his part time shift at the Motel 6 at one end of the strip. The most beautiful woman in the world walked in looking for a room for the weekend. Her name was Michelle McCormack. She was a blond with blue eyes with glasses. She had those fancy transitions lenses. When John found his tongue again he tried to compliment her on her glasses. For the next three days they spent every minute together.

The manager came over and told John to give Michelle Room 12 at the end of the hall. He had to bring Michelle's bags to the room. When they arrived there Michelle asked where to eat. John told her to eat at the Burger King two doors down. Michelle revealed that this was a spur of the moment idea for a trip. She came in from Denver, Colorado.

John asked: "What airline did you use to get here?"

Michelle said: "I only fly Delta. One time I actually flew overseas to Ireland. The food on that flight was more than heavenly."

John asked: "What did you get on that flight?"

Michelle said: "We had beef, potatoes, and carrots and peas. This time I flew Delta. We don't get a meal on such a short flight. It was only two hours. We got snacks instead. I always get the pretzels and ginger ale. Surprisingly they had chocolate chip cookies this time. Iw ill eat those anytime."

John asked: "Have you ever been to the Grand Canyon?"

Michelle said: "No. Traveling is not really my forte. Las Vegas has plenty of places to eat. I am going back home on Tuesday. I have to go back to work on Wednseday."

John asked: "What do you do for a living?"

Michelle said: "I am a receptionist for a dentist. I had to call him for a year and then I had to practically hire myself for the job. He never returned my call. He doesn't like me, but I have been there for twenty five years now. I think he just tolerates my existence to make appointments and answer his phones."

John asked: "Are you happy there?"

Michelle said: "It is a job. It pays the rent and I have health insurance. God knows I need it. I am getting older now and things are starting to go wrong with my insides."

John asked: "Can you bear children?"

Michelle said: "Probably. But with my medications it might not be such a good idea. The patients seem to like me. Since I started we have had maybe 2% cancellation rate. Everybody opens up to me. They now when I do the paperwork it is time to not talk to me."

John asked: "Would you consider marrying me?"

Michelle asked: "What do you do besides being a receptionist at a motel?"

John said: "I am a detective during the week with the Las Vegas Police department. Whenever we are on a case there are long hours out of the house. I might be called out in the middle of the night. We are between cases right now. When we are not busy I am on the strip guard duty with my horse Commissioner. We have been together for maybe three years now."

Michelle asked: "Can you add me to your health insurance?"

John said: "Yes. I can do that. It might be a month or so before it takes place. People have to make phone calls and money has to get into the computer."

Michelle asked: "What kind of wedding would you like?"

John said: "I would like to have a big church wedding. The police department has a very special relationship with my pastor of St. Peter's Church. If a cop is shot on the job or something he is on call for counseling."

Michelle asked: "When can we get married?"

John said: "The Catholic Church wants to have six months of pre-Cannon Instruction. That means December at the earliest. May I suggest a Christmas Eve Wedding?"

Michelle's eyes lit up like a Christmas Tree and said Oh Boy!! That would be different. We would never forget our anniversary then."

John said: "Go back to Colorado when your airline ticket says so. Leave me your phone number so I can call you. Also, leave me your e-mail address."

Michelle said: "One thing that is important to me is that the wedding cake has to be perfect. I want a 3 tier yellow cake. One layer chocolate filling, one layer vanilla filling, and one layer lemon filling. The outside should be white frosting with roses on the outside. If you want a grooms cake feel free to buy that one too."

John asked: "Hold it right there Michelle. Please explain the concept of a groom's cake."

Michelle said: "That signifies something that speaks of you personally. You are a cop, so it would be in the shape of a police badge. You are a mounted cop, so the alternative would be a cake in the shape of a horse. The filling would be your favorite."

John said: "Got it ma'am. I will take care of the details."

Michelle said: "One more thing John. Whether you buy your tuxedo or rent it is your decision. I want you to have your cumberbund the same color as your tie and vest. This is your wedding also. I want you to have some say in it." John saluted her and said: "I I Captain. You will not regret it for a minute. I promise you this will be the best wedding you ever dreamed of." With that Michelle arrived at the airport and boarded the plane home to Denver.

CHAPTER 2

The next day Tuesday John arrived at the precinct for work. He busted down Robert's door and nearly knocked Norman out of his chair. He interrupted a meeting between Robert and the police commissioner.

Robert said: "Calm down John. Just sit down and tell us all about what is on your mind." He just then noticed Norman sitting there watching the spectacle.

John said: "Oh good morning sir. I apologize for interrupting your meeting. It has just been one of those exciting weekends."

Norman said: "What happened? Please share with the class."

John said: "I am in love!!! I am getting married.!!!"

Norman asked: "How long have you known this girl?"

John said: "Three days. We have a lot in common. We seem to be the perfect match. She is looking for a husband but not too much interest in children/ I can go children or no children either way. I will let her be in charge of our sex life. She is letting me get the wedding details together. She left me her instructions."

Norman asked; "What kind of wedding do you want?"

John said: "We want a church wedding with Father Raaser presiding. I will have to talk to him on Saturday."

Robert asked: "What about groomsmen?"

John said: "I was hoping you could be my best man and Norman and Ronald be my groomsmen. All 3 of you are married so your wives can be the ladies coming down the aisle."

Robert called Ronald on the phone and asked if he would be willing to do it. Ronald jumped at that chance without thinking. Him and Eloise will be there with bells on. If this new wife needs any help Eloise can be of assistance in any way possible."

Norman said: "You are between cases right now. Take Commissioner the horse and wander around the strip for your shift. Don't forget to drink your water and water the horse down constantly. Try to walk in the shade as much as possible. Now off with you. Go!!!"

CHAPTER 3

Nothing much happened on the job during that week. It was blessedly quiet. The horse liked to stop and watch the Roller Coaster move. John ran into the usual tourists who wanted a picture with the horse. Kids love it. It was hard to tell who was having more fun. John, the tourists, or the horse.

On Saturday before Mass John walked into the sacristy to talk to Father Raaser. He was delighted to marry John. John had to explain that his wife to be lives in Colorado.

Father Raaser asked: "Do you know about the six months advance notice for Bans of Marriage?"

John said: "Yes sir. I don't know what pre-Cannon instruction is, but you will have to guide me."

Father Raaser asked: "Do you have a reception place booked yet?"

John said: "I have never thought about that. What should I do?"

Father Raaser said: "I have an alternative in mind. How many guests are you looking at?"

John said: "I don't know. We haven't talked about that yet. So far we have 2 groomsmen and their wives. My best man is also coming with his wife."

Father Raaser asked: "How about 1:00 in the afternoon? We have to get ready for midnight Mass that evening."

John said: "1:00 p.m. sounds perfect. We can have the hall between 2:30-7:00 p.m. My bride said she is not a night person. I want a high mass with the whole incense and everything. She misses that from her childhood."

Father Raaser said; "Consider it done. I can write that down in the book. Now we really need to start Mass before people start walking out." They left the sacristy and started Mass. John would barely get focused on the Mass because he kept daydreaming. On the following Monday John went to the horse stables and got Commissioner. Commissioner stopped dead in his tracks and wouldn't move. John thought he sensed the heat coming of the day. The guard Andrew had to stop John and show him what was wrong with Commissioner. He forgot to dress him. He won't leave the stables without a saddle or bridle.

John said: "OOPPSS!! My apologies Commissioner. My head is elsewhere today."

Andrew said: "Bring the extra pail of water to cool him down. He will need that and so will you."

John said: "If I give him too much to drink he will pee on the strip. Horses aren't covered like humans are."

Andrew said: "Direct him to the gutter where people don't walk."

John asked: "What do I do if I have to suddenly pee?"

Andrew said: "Get on your radio and call for another cop. Remember to use the codes. The whole department doesn't have to hear a direct statement that you have to pee. Above all don't you dare leave him unattended." When John left Andrew had to call Robert to warn him that John wasn't active quite right today. He was on speaker phone in Robert's office. Norman put out a directive to everyone that John was in love. Just don't leave him alone for too long. Keep an eye on him. Norman directed Mitchell Banks to ride along with John to make sure he doesn't hurt himself. Mitchell found John and they spent the whole shift together.

CHAPTER 4

Over the next six months John endured the pre-Cannon instruction. Each meeting was scheduled for a Saturday or a Sunday afternoon so it doesn't conflict with his jobs working hours. On the Sunday before Thanksgiving Michelle called John to ask if she could move in before Thanksgiving. Her boss died and she was out of a job. She did not want to go through the hassle of unemployment when she knew she was leaving the state in about a month. John was overjoyed to see her again. The day before Thanksgiving she landed at McCarren airport at the Delta terminal. Unfortunately she had to take a cab to John's house because he was still at work. She called him when she got there and they met an hour later. She went to the corner diner to get refreshed. When she finished she returned to John's house and eh was just coming home. They embraced and kissed lovingly. The couldn't stop embracing. John had to control himself to wait another few weeks.

John asked: "How was your flight?"

Michelle said: "It was smooth. Not much turbulence. After a while I took my sweater off of my face and got up the courage to open my eyes. That wasn't until the pilot said we were free to walk around the aisles. We were level by then. I am too claustophobic. I got up to walk around and I felt better. I met some nice people. We looked out the window together and saw the Grand Canyon. I saw the snow caps on top of the Colorado Rockies. Up in there the snow never melts. People are always challenging themselves to see how far they can get to the top. Every year there is at least one to five deaths. One time somebody came upon just a skeleton. He investigated the area and found there was a parachute nearby. The clothing was identified from the 1940's. Miraculously he had his ID on him. It looked like he parachuted out of an airplane an got tangled up in something. He was buried right were he was and a cross was fashioned from some wood. There wasn't much hope of finding his family anymore. They did a final Act of Contrition for the repose of his soul. Too bad there wasn't a priest around to give him last rights."

John said: "Let me give you the schedule for tomorrow. We have 9:00 Mass at St. Peter's. That is where we are getting married. The pastor is the one who will marry us. My parish does a blessing of the food tomorrow morning. We will talk to him after Mass. He wants to do at least one session of pre-Cannon instruction with you."

Michelle said: "I have never did pre-Cannon instruction before. He will have to guide me through it."

John said: "Don't worry about it. I didn't know about it either until he did it with me." During Thanksgiving Mass Norman secretly sent a text message to the whole guest list for John's wedding. He had a dream that something terrible happened at the reception. The text stated that everybody should bring their guns and badges to the wedding. He sat in the last pew, so nobody looked over his shoulder. He did it right when the priest did the blessing of the food.

CHAPTER 5

At the end of the Mass John and Michelle went into the sacristy to meet with Father Raaser. He greeted them with a smile on his face and said: "Please follow me into the rectory. I will get you a cup of coffee and then we can talk. We shall go down the back stairs. They went down the back stairs and down the hallway. Then up another flight. It was the way priests went from the rectory to the church without actually leaving the building. It was the way the priests took even when it rained. Father Raaser found it quite by accident. He couldn't sleep one night, so he went about exploring. They were settled in the counseling room at the front of the rectory. It had the name Zaccharia's room. Each room in the rectory was named after a biblical character. Everybody in the rectory supported the idea. Zaccharia was Father Raaser's favorite character. Father Raaser reappeared with a tray of coffee mugs and buttered rolls. It was a little early for cake and cookies.

When they finished they were ready to begin. Father Raaser said: "So. This is the last session before the wedding. I understand John has been doing most of the work."

Michelle said: "Yes sir. I just moved here from Colorado. I arrived yesterday. I was originally planning to wait until December, but I lost my job unexpectedly. I didn't want the hassle of dealing with unemployment, so I just packed up one suitcase and came here early."

Father Raaser asked: "Where do you stand on producing children?"

Michelle said: "I could probably have them, but with all my medications it might not be such a good idea. I am afraid of side effects to the embryo."

Father Raaser asked: "Do you understand that if it is in the cards God will take care of the embryo?"

Michelle said: "Yes sir. I do understand that."

Father Raaser asked: "Are you willing to wait until you are married to even try?"

Michelle said: "Yes sir. I am still untouched in that fashion."

Father Raaser asked; "If you have a healthy baby are you willing to have it Baptized into the Catholic Church?"

Michelle said: "Yes sir. I have been religious and church going all my life."

Father Raaser asked: "Have you talked about money and sharing a checking account and a savings account?"

Michelle said: "No sir. We haven't touched that subject yet."

Father Raaser spoke to John and said: "See to it that that is settled before the wedding."

John said: "Yes sir. It will be done."

Father Raaser said: "Well now. I guess we have concluded all there is to this Pre-Cannon Instruction business. John, you have work in an hours. So far you have not allowed this wedding to interfere with your work. Don't mess up now. Now I must excuse myself for the day. Other Business to attend to." They all stood and outside waiting for them was Robert Schapiro. Robert made a phone call and got John the day off. He was glad to do it. Robert gave them a lift to his house to meet his wife Joyce. Waiting for them there were Ronald and Eloise and their four year old daughter Arlene. They were expecting Sr.

Angelus pretty soon to make an appearance. They spent the day getting to know each other. Norman and his wife also showed up. The real purpose for this gathering was not only Thanksgiving Dinner, but also to get to knew each other. This was after all the wedding party. John said: "Do not be frightened Michelle. By the end of the day these three cackling hens will know your blood type."

Michelle asked: "Did you arrange this the whole time?"

John laughed and said: "Of course I did."

CHAPTER 6

They arrived at Robert's house and introduced Michelle to Joyce and the rest of the wives. When Michelle finished shaking hands with everybody the gentlemen retired to the living room. The ladies stayed in the kitchen.

Joyce said: "So Michelle. Let me give you the low down on everybody. We are all cops' wives except for Eloise. This is Ronald's wife. Ronald is the only one who isn't a cop. Ronald was the altar boy partner of my husband Robert. They parted and then reunited years later. We are all one bog happy family. Our husbands all work together and are on the same squad. Two members of the squad are not here today. They had their own plans for the holiday. John wanted us to be part of your wedding party. We will be standing on your side and our husbands will be standing next to John. John is also alone in the world. He is like the son we never had. We are just waiting for one more guest. Sr. Angelus is her name. She should be here very shortly. When she gets here we will turn off the turkey and mashed potatoes. Before we sit down everybody stands behind the chairs and Robert says Grace of Thanks. Then we all sit down. The food is passed around and you eat whatever you want. You will catch on to us pretty quickly." On that note the front door bell rang. It was Sr. Angelus. She entered the kitchen and everybody rose in greeting. Michelle introduced herself. She entered the living room and all the gentlemen rose in greeting. Joyce got busy with the turkey and Robert came in to work the mixer for the mashed potatoes. Everybody helped serve and put the food on the table.

Michelle asked: "Excuse me Joyce. Do we have assigned places?"

Joyce said: "No. We just have seats and feel free to sit anywhere."

Michelle said: "I hope I don't sound stupid by that question. My grandmother had place cards on the table."

Joyce said: "You should never feel stupid about any kind of question. You should hear what comes out of my mouth at work. We are all here to help each other." When the food was ready Robert was summoned to the kitchen to carve the turkey. The ladies brought out the carrots and cranberry sauce. Michelle learned how to use an electric can opener. She announced that she wanted one of those for a wedding present. When everybody was ready they went into the dining room and stood behind the chairs.

Robert said a prayer of thanks. "Bless us oh Lord and these thy gifts which we are about to receive through Christ Our Lord Amen."

Everybody responded "Amen" Everybody sat down and the meal began.

Sr. Angelus asked: "So Michelle. Where are you from?"

Michelle said: "I am from Denver, Colorado originally. I have lived there all my life. I relocated to Nevada a month earlier than expected. My boss died in his sleep and I was out of a job. I didn't want to deal with unemployment for just one month."

Sr. Angelus asked: "Do you have any family?"

Michelle said: "I have family in New York. I hope they can fly out for the wedding. My brother died September 11th. Nobody ever found his body. For all we know he could be hiding somewhere under a different name."

Sr. Angelus asked: "What about your parents?"

Michelle said; "Both have passed on."

Robert said: "John, Father Raaser spoke to me yesterday. Sr. Angelus and Father Raaser will be the witnesses to this marriage."

Michelle said: "I thought the wedding party were the witnesses?"

John said: "That is what I thought too."

Robert said: "Don't look at me. I have been trying to remember my own wedding. I can't remember the church details."

Sr. Angelus said: "I was there at all three of your weddings. As a guest I have never been asked to be a witness to anything. A witness signs the wedding certificate. That is usually the Best Man and Maid of Honor. You approach the altar and the witnesses sign the paper during the Mass. Then you are officially married cross your fingers until death do you part."

Norman's cell phone rang off and everybody had naughty words going through their heads. It was luckily unrelated to work. They were all afraid a case came up. It was just his mother wishing him a blessed day. Everybody said "Whew. That was a close one."

John said: "Michelle, over the next four weeks you will be spending a lot of time with these ladies.

They will help you with the details of the female end of the wedding."

Michelle asked: "What do you mean female end of the wedding?"

John said: "Your dress and flowers. That is your part. The gentlemen end is the tuxedos."

CHAPTER 7

After dinner the gentlemen cleared the table and did the dishes. All the extra food was put into Tupperware bowls and sent home with the leftovers. Robert washed the dishes and Ronald dried the dishes. John and Norman put them away. By the time they were done the kitchen was spotless. Robert even mopped the floor. The kitchen was full of guy talk. They weren't at work, so they were free to scratch themselves if they felt like it. Nobody took up the practice of swearing. Norman wasn't afraid to lit it out, but not when he was a guest in someone else's house. When he left he let it all out. Really he was just mad at his wife for what she said and the way she afted at the table. He never liked it when she slouched. The one thing they never did was drink alcohol. They never knew when they were going to get called out on a murder scene or anything. Everybody had to be clean of drugs and alcohol. Norman's wife put up with the cursing only to have a husband who never drank.

The ladies in the meantime adjourned to the living room for their own hen session. Joyce got out a notebook and pen and decided to make a list of what needed to be done for the wedding. Step number one was to buy the dress and veil. Step number two was to buy the flowers or at least to pick them out first. Place the order early. John took care of the rings. He already brought them on lay away. John's job was also to make the final arrangements for the reception hall. Joyce came up with an alternative site just in case the convention hall burned down or some other tragedy. She said: "Leave that to me. If the time comes follow me. I will be the leader." Everybody agreed to that plan.

Eloise asked: "Do you want John to see your dress or you before the wedding?"

Michelle said: "No. I want to follow that tradition to the letter. Please don't let him see me until I walk down the aisle."

Joyce asked: "How do you feel about horses?"

Michelle said: "I love horses with all my heart. I think they are the most beautiful creatures of God's creation."

Joyce asked: "Have you ever been horseback riding?"

Michelle said: "No. That is the one thing I always wanted to do."

Robert was eavesdropping from the kitchen. He asked: "Have you ever met Commissioner the Horse, John's partner?"

Michelle said: "No. But since I am not a cop I don't think I can get near them." Robert walked back into the kitchen and said: "John, I have an idea that you can do. Leave it to me and it will be revealed to you when the time is right. Robert liked to talk in clipped ideas and not whole thoughts. John just dismissed it and let Robert think through whatever he had on his mind. At the end of the evening everybody said good bye and wished Michelle good luck. They already welcomed her into the fold as a member of the family. The ladies made an appointment with Michelle to go dress shopping two days later. That night when they were in bed Robert said; "Joyce, I was eavesdropping today.

I heard you ask Michelle about her love of horses. I have an idea that will make her pee her pants and probably you will do something else unsightly." Joyce kicked Robert out of the bed for that. She said: "You sleep on the floor for that. John is a good friend of yours and if you do anything to embarrass him I promise you will regret this because you will be sleeping on the floor. Sp spill the beans. What is your plan?"

Robert said: "I am going to bring Commissioner the Horse to the church. I will arrange it with Andrew for transport and Michelle will ride up the aisle on him."

Joyce asked: "Are you crazy? What exactly have you been drinking?"

Robert said; "It is the perfect plan. John is very attached to the horse and Michelle love horses. It would be a nice surprise for John."

Joyce said; "Call me old fashioned, but I thought one of you guys would be walking her down the aisle like anyone else?"

Robert said; "We will. This is just a bonus treat for John as well as Michelle. And don't you dare and tell anyone about it."

Joyce said: "This whole plan is absurd and probably against the health code, but on the other hand I love it. Does Norman approve of you using police equipment for non police work?"

Robert said: "I haven't told him yet. But he should be fine with it."

Joyce said; "The only reason you are not sleeping in the recliner tonight is because I think it is a good idea. God help us all if something happens. I have work in the morning, so good night."

After she turned over Robert shook her and said: "One more thing honey. I am bringing Daisy to the wedding also as a surprise. I will go to Pet Smart and buy her a wedding gown made for dogs. She is after all a female dog."

Joyce kicked him out of bed and said: "Sleep on the floor tonight."

CHAPTER 8

John and Michelle arrived home just before 7:00 that evening. John had to stop at the 7-11 for evening snacks.

Michelle said: "Seriously John. After all the food we ate today you want more snacks just before bed time?"

John said; "I already went to the toilet, so now I am all empty. I have to get a refill so my stomach doesn't get bored with nothing to do."

As Michelle started putting the ood away she decided to put water on for tea. She asked: "John, do you want some tea? That would push more stuff through and out."

John said: "Yes. Good idea. Then we can have the chocolate chip cookies. What made you put them in the refrigerator?"

Michelle said: "I always do that. They taste better that way."

John asked: "So. What do you think of our little group?"

Michelle said: "I think I am going to like being here. They all seemed more than willing to welcome me into the fold."

John asked: "Are you Scottish by the way?"

Michelle said: "I am part Scottish and part Irish. How did you happen to pick that up?"

John said: "It was that phrase you used. Welcoming you into the fold is part of the Scottish Wedding Ceremony. My grandparents were from England. I also did a term paper in high school about Scotland. That phrase came up in my research."

Michelle asked: "Do you want to use that in the ceremony?"

John said: "I will try, but I can't promise that will work out." The next day John and all his squad had off. He went to the Motel 6 to work instead. He didn't want to be paying the bills for the wedding for too long. The two cakes were already paid off, so that was one thing less to worry about. He put most of his free time into working. When he got to the Motel 6 he called Michelle and asked: "By the way Michelle. What are your plans for today?"

Michelle said: "For today I will stay home and unpack and get to know your cat. I noticed he was snooping in my things already. You forgot to mention you had one. I caught him on my bed. Tomorrow I will go dress shopping with the girls."

John said: "Have a nice day Michelle. I should be home about six o'clock. Don't let the cat out of the house."

CHAPTER 9

On Saturday all the gentlemen drove their wives to Robert's house. The gentlemen went to John's house to wait for him to come home. He came home around 3"00 in the afternoon. By that time Robert made a phone call to the limo company. Only one more preparation was needed and that was the tuxedoes. All the gentlemen tried theirs on at home so that all fit still. John needed to buy his own tuxedo. The other gentlemen had red ties and cumberbunt. It was apparently the best color for them. They took off for the florist to get flowers the same color as the cumberbundt. Luckily the florist had the perfect match in color. Once that was done there was nothing left to do but to wait three weeks for the wedding. Before the gentlemen left John instructed them to take the bus so that they can point out points of interest to Michelle. They went to a store named Martha's Wedding Dress. They passed the DMV and the court house.

Finally they arrived at the dress shop right in the heart of downtown Las Vegas. It was called Martha's Dress Shop. All of them were customers there. Martha came out to greet the group.

Martha said: "Good morning ladies. It is good to see you again."

Joyce said: "Good morning Martha. We brought you a new customer. She is the wife to be of John, the new member of the squad. He has been there for about two years now. He is still the baby of the group. By the way. How is business in this economy?"

Martha said: "Business is pretty good, but yesterday was a raving nightmare. We had the worst bridezilla in here that we never thought was possible.

Michelle asked; "You mean even worse than those on the show?"

Martha said: "Yes. She was even worse than that. I never thought that was possible. She just kept cursing and swearing up a blue streak. She gained weight after we did alterations on her dress. It didn't fit so somehow that was our fault."

Michelle said: "I guess you meet all kinds of people in this business."

Martha asked: "What kind of dress were you looking for?"

Michelle said: "I like beading and sparkles."

Martha asked: "What is your usual dress size?"

Michelle said: "I think it is about a size 10, but normally I wear pant suits."

Martha said: "Size 10 converts to approximately size 14. Wedding dresses are cut and sized differently. Don't worry about the size. First go for the style. We do alterations."

Michelle asked: "What are alterations?"

Martha said: "We take it in here and add material there and make it bigger there. We also sometimes hem up the length." After trying on several dresses she picked out the perfect one. It had everything she wanted. It didn't even need too much alterations.

Martha said: "You want it a little big because of the issue of eating and dancing. There is nothing worse than trying to eat with a tight dress on all day. By the way. You can't wear a bra with this dress."

Michelle almost hit the ceiling when she said "WHAT!!!?"

Martha laughed and said: "Relax. We have special underclothes for that. Also, we have the bra sewn into the dress. All of your friends have worn this. They will help you squirm into it."

Joyce said: It is called a camasol. That is a one piece. We will help you get into it. John can help you get out of it."

Martha said: "Take this one piece into the dressing room. Try it on. Keep your panties on. Believe it or not some people do take their panties off and try it on. We cannot sell them or give them away for obvious reasons. We have to throw them out. We lose a lot of money that way. Normally we have to instruct every customer on that issue. I promise I wasn't being funny telling you that."

Michelle said: "Don't worry about it. I am glad to told me that clue." After she went in there she struggled into the undergarment. Joyce went inside and tied it in the back. Michelle said it was a perfect fit. Then she picked out the dress. After three dresses she picked out the right one for her. It had everything she was looking for in a dress. She brought a sparkly belt to go around the waist. Joyce brought the dress on her credit card and when the bill came it was split four ways. Michelle paid for her own camasol. It was a rather personal item.

CHAPTER 10

That night John came home around 6:30. He said: "So. How was your day?"

Michelle said: "It was wonderful. I brought the dress and camasol."

John asked: "What is a camasol?"

Michelle said: "My undergarments. It is the bra and panties in one piece."

John said: "Sorry I asked. Did you play with my cat today?"

Michelle said: "Yes. The first time we met he was walking around with my panties in his mouth. I chased him and he thought I was playing. He hasn't left my side since then."

John said: "I am jealous. He never stole my panties like that."

Michelle asked: "What about the limo and tuxedoes?"

John said: "The limo and tuxes are all finished with. We just are waiting for Dec. 24th to come around. Please do me one favor. Don't look at the tux before that. I want you to be surprised."

Michelle said; "Fair enough. I can follow that. My dress is at Joyce and Robert's house. I didn't want you to snoop and look at it."

CHAPTER 11

Joyce and Robert were settling in for a relaxing evening. Robert asked: "How was your day with the ladies?"

Joyce said: "Very successful. Michelle managed to buy a dress. It was the third one she tried on. It is hanging in our closet. It felt good to see Martha again."

Robert asked: "May I take a peek at the dress?"

Joyce said: "Okay. But don't you dare describe it to anyone. Especially to John. Not seeing the dress is extremely urgent to follow. Don't even open your mouth about it." Robert looked at it and it was breathtaking. He couldn't wait to see Michelle in that dress. They went to bed early and the dog joined them. They woke early and walked the dog together. They both slept deeply all night. The dog woke up Robert by licking him in the face. It was time for a walk. The dog never let Robert sleep. Joyce had to leave Robert to get ready for work. Robert had to spend the day making the final arrangements for the wedding. That was an adventure. The hall was set up, the cake was picked up. Everything seemed to be right on schedule. There was nothing left to do. The night before the wedding all the gentlemen slept in John's house and all the ladies slept at Joyce's house. John couldn't sleep and neither could Norman. He was worried about his extra special surprise coming in the morning. Joyce couldn't sleep because of the excitement of the day.

CHAPTER 12

The limp picked up the gentlemen right at 12:00 noon just as scheduled. It was a white limo, a stretch kind of limo. It had a TV and stereo inside and plenty of water and pretzels. The limo driver told the gentlemen to make sure to eat plenty of pretzels so they don't pass out from hunger. Father Raaser would have none of that fainting bid in his church. Luckily nobody got stupidly drunk the night before. Father Raaser related that story to them that happened. Apparently he was just a teenager who got drunk and the grown ups in charge of him gave him too much. He was treated for alcohol poisoning. Everybody ate a hearty breakfast in the corner diner. That was very important to them.

The ladies woke up to a very similar morning routine. Breakfast at the corner diner. They were there by 6:00 because they had make-up to do. They were finished and out the door by 7:30. No gallivanting around. At 8:30 they started their own make up. At 10:30 everybody was finished and it was time to get the dresses on. They were interrupted by a knock on the door. It was a neighbor requesting from Robert to bring the dog out. Robert spoke to Joyce on the phone and handed Daisy over without question. Joyce still wasn't sure why, but she didn't have time to argue.

Michelle asked: "Who was at the door?"

Joyce said: "It was a neighbor. For some reason Robert wants me to give the dog to him. I don't know what Robert is thinking. I don't have time to think about it. Now onto the most important part of the day. We need to wiggle you into the wedding dress. First take your panties off and put on the camasol."

Michelle said: "I am a rebel. I will wear this thing with my panties."

Eloise said: "Fine Michelle. Whatever makes you comfortable."

Michelle said: "With this tie in the back I will take my bra off." She did so and with much pulling and giggling and breathing hard they were done with that. That was the hardest part of getting dressed. The wedding dress was the most fun. She had to step into it and pull it up. The girls tied it in the back. It was awkward to have it on. Michelle knew it was just for one day. She turned it into a learning experience. It didn't take too long to get dressed. She always imagined it as an all day 8 hour affair. Finally at 12:00 noon the limo pulled up. Everybody entered and they were in awe struck at the inside. It was pink on the outside and had a TV and stereo and plenty of water stored in the limo. The driver explained that the other white limo was out for repairs, so they sent the pink one instead. When they entered Michelle said: "St. Peter's Church Please." The limo driver laughed and said: "Yes madam." They were not late because it was made clear that lateness could not happen. They had to get the church ready for Christmas Eve festivities. Everybody arrived at the church in one piece and on time.

CHAPTER 13

Father Raaser met the gentlemen at the front door of the church. They were all descent looking with straight ties and clean hands and white shirts. They passed inspection for entry to God's House. Suddenly Father Raaser exploded and said: "HOLD IT ROBERT!!!"

Robert asked: "What is it sir?"

Father Raaser said: "What in tarnation is Daisy doing here?"

Robert said: "Everybody loves Daisy. I thought she could be a part of this too. It is a special surprise for John."

Father Raaser said: "Fine. I relent. I was just surprised to see a dog at a wedding. It is not something you see everyday."

Norman said: "AH! Excuse me sir. I also have a surprise for John. I will wait here for the ladies and direct traffic. We all have to wait here anyway to walk down the aisle.

Father Raaser said: "If you bring Commissioner the Horse down here I promise I will eat that Unity Candle."

Sr. Angelus was watching the spectacle and seemed to appear out of nowhere. She interrupted and said: "Please forgive Father Raaser for his outburst. I don't think he has been sleeping well. It is the pressure of the holidays getting to him." Norman's cell phone rang just has the limo pulled up. John didn't know what was going on in the back because Ronald directed him to stand in front of the altar and wait. Father Raaser went into the sacristy to get his alb on. Sr. Angelus came up and told John to sit down on the alter steps until she gets a signal otherwise.

Sr. Angelus said: "The gang is working on a surprise for you. Actually 2 surprises. Just be patient and do as you are told."

John smiled and said: "Do you really know what is going on?"

Sr. Angelus said: "Yes I do, but go with the flow. The squad is working hard to make this a nice day for you. Smile through it. Enjoy it because there will never be another one like it." Father Raaser came out just as Sr. Angelus got the signal that all was ready to begin. He took his place right next to John. They were facing each other. Sr. Angelus sat back down in the pews. There was a scattering of parishioners who were asked to show up and be witnesses. Some sat on the bride's side and some sat on the groom's side. They were instructed to wear their best dress and full formal regalia.

John asked: "Who are these people sir?"

Father Raaser said: "There are parishioners of ours. I asked them here because we need witnesses. I told them to wear their full formal regalia. Just smile at them and don't look like you are about to vomit." John did his best not to look rather green around the gills. Finally the ladies showed up. Normal helped them out one by one. Michelle came out last. They all assembled with their husbands and lined up. When they looked in the church it was half full with people. The precinct came in a side door and assembled at the front of each pew. They reminded Michelle of color guards. At the front was two flags. The American flag an the Vatican Flag, also called the Flag of the Keeper. It was designed by the Vatican. The music was cued and the assembled started down the aisle. First there was Arlene being the flower girl. Then Robert and Joyce. Norman and his wife was next. Then Ronald and Eloise. They all made it down the aisle in one piece. Nobody tripped or anything like that. Robert made a second trip down the aisle with Michelle at his arm. She made it to the altar and gave her arm to John. He took her to he rest of the way. Robert shook hands with John and gave Michelle a kiss on the cheek.

Father Raaser asked: "Are we ready?"

Norman said: "No sir. There is just one guest who isn't here yet. He is stuck in traffic. He should be here momentarily. We need to wait for his arrival."

John said: "Excuse me sir. Father Raaser has to get ready for tonight."

Norman said: "He should be here momentarily. I think I see him now."

Robert said; "Zip it John. Don't talk back to people." It was then that Michelle noticed Daisy the Beagle dog watching the spectacle. She squealed out in delight that the dog made an appearance. She picked up her head and barked once and got all excited. She started wagging her tail. She looked down the aisle and sure as the day there was Commissioner the Horse making an appearance. He started his trek down the aisle and stood right next to the gentlemen of the wedding party. John and Michelle both squealed in delight. John was in awe the rest of the day. He didn't know how to thank everyone for doing this for them. The ceremony began and nobody heard a peep out of either the horse or the dog the rest of the day. There were no mishaps. A few giggles when the bride and groom were incensed and Daisy and the Horse both sneezed. Arlene also sneezed, but she tried to be a polite lady about it. The ceremony concluded and everybody started down the aisle. All the color guards and the cops took out their swords and criss crossed them together. Then theat was the signal to start. AT the back of the church everybody piled in to one limo. They made one stop in Robert's house to drop off the dog. She wasn't allowed at the reception hall. Simon rode Commissioner to the strip and then got back to the horse stables. He needed a few words of encouragement from John. Then he was good to go.

CHAPTER 14

The reception hall was magnificent. It was decorated with balloons and each table had a flower on it. It was free seating. People were surprised to see no place cards. When the squad made their appearance they walked in. When the bride and groom made their appearance everybody stood and applauded. Michelle took the microphone and said: "John and I would like to thank you all for coming out this afternoon. It has been a fairly easy road to travel. I had plenty of help from the wives. The Las Vegas Police Department has already welcomed me into the group. I am the newest member of the wives group. I was shocked to see Commissioner the Horse clopping down the aisle. You guys sure are the best. For those of you who don't know this about me I am a lover of animals. Dinner will now be served because we have the hall until 5:30. We would also like to wish you all a Merry Christmas."

Just then everybody heard a pop. Michelle asked: "What was that?"

Simon yelled: "Gunshots!!!" Everybody down!!!" The gentlemen jumped on top of their wives. John jumped on top of Sr. Angelus. When the gunshots stopped everybody stood and yelled: "What happened!!!":

Norman took the microphone and said: "All Cops stand up here in a line horizontally." They all did as they were told. Within a microsecond everybody was up there. Norman took each person's gun and looked at it. He was checking to see if any of them were fired just a few minutes ago. Luckily none were.

Eloise and Joyce brought Michelle over to their table for a nice cold drink of water. What she really needed was the plate of Roast Beef to fill her stomach. The next time she looked up was to see Robert coming out of the kitchen with somebody in handcuffs. The gun was in a zip lock plastic bag. He had to improvise because he didn't have a formal evidence bag. That was not something to carry to a wedding. He gave the gun to Norman and sure enough it smelled of recently being fired. Robert asked: "Michelle, do you know this person?"

Michelle shrieked: "OH MY GOD!! WHAT IN GOD'S HOLY TARNATION ARE YOU DOING HERE??!!

John asked: "Who is this man Michelle?"

Michelle said: "If I didn't know nay better I'd say that was my long lost brother!!"

John asked: "Is that right?"

The man said: "Yes sir. I am."

Norman asked: "What is your name?"

The man said: "My name is Donald."

Norman asked: "Do you realize I have to arrest you now?"

Donald said; "Yes sir."

Norman said; "You have a right to remain silent. Anything you do say can and will be used against you in a court of law. You have a right to an attorney. If you cannot afford one one will be appointed for you. Do you understand these rights as I have read them to you?"

Donald said: "Yes sir. I do."

Norman said: "Let me take you down to the precinct. We will talk there. Simon will accompany me to process him into the system."

Robert said: "Excuse me sir. We need to call for a bus because one person was shot in the hip." Just then the paramedics showed up and were escorted into the kitchen.

CHAPTER 15

When Donald arrived at the police precinct he was processed immediately. He had his picture taken, his fingerprints taken and his shoes taken away from him. He was taken to a holding cell temporarily. There was a cop who was assigned to make sure he doesn't escape. Luckily he was the only prisoner. Donald laughed so hard it loked like he was about to ruptue something in his brain. The cop sent to guard him looked barely eighteen years old. He had such a baby face Donald thought he was maybe fifteen years old. His true age was twenty five. He knew all the tricks prisoners use to get out. He had to escort them to the bathroom and watch as they did their business. A year after he started the precinct installed a toilet right in the cage. There was just no curtain for privacy. Everybody walking by could see what he was doing. There was no window to look out of.

Norman came by after about an hour to inform Donald that his shooting victim would live. That meant that the charges would be attempted murder and carrying a concealed weapon. That carries a sentence fo five years or less. He was taken to an interrogation room for an interview. Out of sight there were four officers witnessing the interrogation. Norman did the actual interrogation. There were no snacks offered because Norman was old school and did not believe in coddling perptrators. After questioning he was indicted for attempted murder.

CHAPTER 16

Meanwhile back at the wedding reception Robert took charge of the rest of the afternoon. They played a game with the bride and groom. They asked questions of the bride and groom. She held up one of his shoes and he held up one of her shoes. Robert asked questions such as who drinks more coffee. Who ahs the bigger appetite etc. There was a lot of laughing during that game. Somehow the kitchen got their act together and served the food. Everybody was happy. Michelle was starving by then. She just gobbled down the whole plate like a vacuum. The manager came out and announced that due to the unusual circumstances the group can have the hall for an extra hour. This way they did not have to inhale the cake. John expressed his gratitude for that. The cake was the most scrumptious and tasty thing they ever had. Michelle had one piece from each tier plus one piece from the groom's cake. He chose to make it in the shape of a policeman. He chose blue icing to match the color of the uniform. Gold buttons and even a gun drawn on the wasteband. This was all done with icing. Michelle and John were both speechless at what people can do with cake nowadays. He decided to have a pound cake. They both almost choked on it. Everybody left on time. Some people didn't stay for cake because they were traveling for Christmas Eve. Robert came out and explained that nobody will leave until the bride and groom leave. The limo drove up right on time and they departed. John and Michelle went to the Flamingo Hotel on the strip. They got the honeymoon suite on the 18th floor. They found complimentary champagne and a fruit bowl on the table. Michelle was so tired it took her an hour to squirm out of her dress and under things and get into a comfortable pair of pajamas. They each had a Diet Pepsi and went straight to sleep by 9:00. John took about a half hour to get out of his tuxedo.

CHAPTER 17

The next day was Christmas Day. They had breakfast in bed.

Michelle asked: "How did you sleep last night?"

John said: "I slept like a log. The last thing I remember was trying to figure out how to get that cumberbunt off. I was so tired I couldn't think of the snaps in the back."

Michelle said: "I don't remember anything either. I remember squirming out of my corset, but don't ask me how. By the way John. Is there any way I could speak to my brother?"

John said: "There might be a problem with that. Let me call Robert and see what we can arrange." John made a call to Robert on his cell phone. Robert answered on the 2nd ring. They greeted each other and then John got down to the real reason he called.

Robert said: "I am not working today. Let me call Norman and see how far he is with being processed."

Robert called Norman and exchanged pleasantries. Then he got down to the question at hand.

Norman said: "I am in the precinct now. I can make a deal with you. I can hold off the procedures until tomorrow. Tell John and Michelle to come down today."

Robert said: "Thank you Norman. I will be sure and pass along this message to them. John told me it was a request from Michelle."

Norman said; "Have a great day Robert. Promise me you will spend it with your wife and dog. Send John and Michelle over to me. I will take care of them."

Robert said: "I will tell them to be there at 12:00 noon." They hung up and Robert called John back. He relayed the message.

CHAPTER 18

John and Michelle arrived right on time and met Norman at the front desk.

Norman asked: "So. How was your wedding night?"

John said: "It was beautiful. We both crashed by 9:00. I remember drinking a soda before bed, but nothing after that."

Norman said: "I can take you to your brother, but after that I will need to talk to you." Michelle was taken to a room with Donald in a cage. Norman explained that he had to have a guard on him around the clock. The guard's name was Nicholas.

Michelle asked: "Has he given you any trouble?"

Nicholas said: "No madam. He has been very quiet and just sat there seething and moping."

Michelle asked: "Where have you been since 9/11?"

Donald said: "I was in a bad marriage. I ran away because I saw it as an opportunity to escape."

Michelle said: "You were declared dead back in 2008. After seven years that is what happens. Your body was never found."

Donald asked: "How did you do that considering you have never been to New York?"

Michelle said: "I did it through a lawyer. You also missed the funerals of both of our parents. Mom was never the same after you vanished like that. It just drove her to her grave. Are you proud of yourself?"

Donald said: "Of course not. Don't be ridiculous."

Michelle asked: "Are you ashamed of yourself?"

Donald said: "Yes. Thoroughly."

Michelle asked: "Do you have any children?"

Donald said: "Yes. Two children. A boy and a girl."

Michelle asked: "How old are they now?"

Donald said: "My daughter is twenty two and my son is twenty one."

Michelle asked: "What are their names?"

Donald said: "Their names are Mark and Nancy."

Michelle asked: "What was your wife's name?"

Donald said: "My wife's name was Melissa."

Michelle asked; "Do you pay alimony and child support?"

Donald said: "No. According to them I am dead. I would rather leave it like that." Michelle didn't notice that Norman and the guard were taking notes.

Norman said: "Excuse me Michelle. There will be a delay until January 4th for the trial. This is because of the holiday. Trial will begin on January 4th. Jury selection will begin and end on January 3rd. We will only need six jurors for this case."

Michelle asked: "What are the charges?"

Norman said: "Attempted murder and carrying a firearm without a permit. Let us adjourn to the next room to talk in private."

CHAPTER 19

They adjourned just as Norman asked. Michelle already got the message that what Norman wants Norman gets.

Norman asked: "What state was Donald born in?"

Michelle said; "We were both born and raised in the state of Colorado."

Norman asked: "When did he mover to New York?"

Michelle said: "He moved out when he was 18 years old. He always had angerf issues. I think he had a fight with my father. He just up and moved. He never contacted us again. It killed my mother of heart break."

Norman asked: "How old is Donald now?"

Michelle said: "He is about 35 years old by now."

Norman asked; "How old are you?"

Michelle said: "I am forty years old now."

Norman asked; "Was he ever reported missing?"

Michelle said; "No. He was legally an adult so we just prayed to God to keep him safe. My mother cried her eyes out the rest of her life. She was never the same."

Norman said; "Thank you for talking to me. I will bring you down to John now."

Michelle asked: "I have one question for you sir. Is he going to stay here for the week?"

Norman said: "Yes. He will eventually be moved to a holding cell with other prisoners. Everything is rather slow around here because of the holiday. He won't need a guard down in holding. It is set up differently. I promise you he will be treated with the utmost respect and dignity."

Michelle asked: "Will I be allowed to visit him downstairs?"

Norman said; "I prefer you not to do that. It will throw the whole system out of whack."

CHAPTER 20

Michelle and John went home for a relaxing day for their first Christmas. They both forgot to buy presents for each other because of the wedding. The gift of a wife was the best Christmas present of all anyway. Michelle felt the same way about getting a husband.

John asked: "Were you able to talk to your brother in private?"

Michelle said: "No. Norman was there and so was a uniformed cop. I felt bad that the cop and Norman had to work on Christmas. There was really no privacy for me to talk to him. They won't take any food."

John said: "It is hard to say no. Sometimes during the domestic disputes people offer us water or a cookie. We are not allowed to accept. We are lucky that the restaurants let us use the bathroom.

That is an advantage of being a cop instead of a civilian citizen."

John said: "By the way. I almost fainted dead away yesterday when I saw Commissioner my horse come klopping the aisle. Father Raaser said that he would personally eat the unity candle if they pulled that off. I am still waiting for that to happen."

Michelle said: "I was also in shock. I almost peed my pants when I saw that. Who's idea was that anyway?"

John said: "It was either Robert or Norman. One of the two. I can't quite pin it down though."

Michelle said: "My brother's trial starts on January 4th. Jury selection will be on January 3rd."

John said: "You will probably be called to testify on his behalf. That means you will be like a character witness. Just remember to tell the truth and don't worry about the outcome. Your brother made his own path in doing what he did. You are not responsible for his actions. I hate to tell you this, but I have to work tomorrow in the Motel 6."

Michelle said: "Don't worry about that. Just go to work and earn a paycheck. I will start looking for work tomorrow along the strip."

John asked: "What areas are you interested in working?"

Michelle said; "Check-in desk and check-out desk."

John said: "Do you know the area of being a butler?"

Michelle said: "I think you work in the hotel suites for the high rollers."

John said: "That is right. You now they have the nerve to make you go to school for that?"

Michelle said: "I heard that. I am not going to school to figure out how to bring somebody's shoes and food. I would flop it down in front of them and tell them to eat." The rest of the day was quiet and uneventful. There were no phone calls coming in. The two of them just curled up on the counch in front of the TV and the cat in between them.

CHAPTER 21

The next day John woke up and Michelle made breakfast. John is a tea drinker, so she drank the whole pot of coffee all by herself. She made a mental note to buy more tea bags for the house. Michelle decided to walk to the strip to get a feel for the place. She took the bus to Freemont street and got a job in the largest souvenir store in the United States. It was a part time job, so but she didn't mind. She told the manager she would be available to substitute if someone call in sick. He was very pleased with the offer. He promised to give her a variety of things to do. Not just work the register. She got her own name tag and everything. She couldn't wait to get home and tell John about it. Her first day was to be January 3rd. Monday, Wednsday, Friday to make it part time. She was always heavily into physical fitness, so walking was second nature to her. By the summer time she will be walking all the way to work. John told her to walk a little bit each day. Then it will be easier for her. Work herself up to it. He told her how proud he was of her that she got a job so soon. John shared a story about an acquaintance of his that had the same kind of luck.

CHAPTER 22

January 3rd rolled around and jury selection began. Twelve jurors were called and six were picked. Nobody tried to get out of it. This wasn't a violet death or anything. The six not picked were sent back to the jury room. It wasn't expected to last very long. The judge's name was Martin O'Neil. The defense attorney's name was Harry O'Connor. The prosecuting attorney's name was Eliot Jones.

Judge O'Neil said: "Good afternoon ladies and gentlemen. Tomorrow we will all assemble right here at 9:00 a.m. We will begin then with opening statements. Lateness will not be tolerated. Your attendance cards will be brought down to the jury room during the day. Just come straight up here."

Everybody listened and did as they were told. Judge O'Neil was not the type of person to cross.

CHAPTER 23

Day 1 of the trial started right on time. Everybody assembled just as instructed.

Judge O'Neil said: "Good morning ladies and gentlemen. Thank you for being punctual this morning. It starts my day off on the right foot. This will be a fairly short trial. It shouldn't be much longer than a week. You will not hear ridiculous questions from the lawyers. The lawyers have a right to object to each other, but I have the final say. I promise they will not be arguing with each other. They know better in my courtroom. With that I ask Eliot Jones to begin with opening statements."

Eliot said: "Thank you your honor. Ladies and gentlemen. I am the prosecuting attorney. My job is to prove to you that Donald did commit this heinous act. It was performed at his sister's wedding two weeks ago."

Judge O'Neil said: "Harry, you may begin with your opening statements."

Harry said: "Thank you your honor. Ladies and gentlemen of the jury. My name is Harry O'Connor. I am the defense attorney. My job is to prove the reason why he did it. When you hear why I am confident you will find him not guilty."

Judge O'Neil said: "Bailiff, please take the attendance cards down to the jury assembly room and inform them that these people are all present and accounted for. Bring the cards back so we can have them tomorrow morning." The bailiff did as he was told.

Judge O'Neil said: "Eliot, call your first witness please."

Eliot said; "I call Norman to the stand." As Norman approached the stand he was sworn in as the witness.

Eliot asked: "What is your occupation?"

Norman said: "I am the chief of police."

Eliot asked: "How did you get involved in this case?"

Norman said: "I was a guest at the wedding. I heard one of my detectives was getting married. I put out a request for other cops to come out and support John in this endeavor. Most of the cops didn't mind coming out on Christmas Eve. It was during the day of Dec. 24th."

Eliot asked: "What about the cops carrying the guns around?"

Norman said: "John and Michelle didn't mind. Some of them were just coming off duty and some were going on duty. Michelle married a cop, but guns don't bother her at all."

Eliot asked: "Was their attendance an order from the boss?"

Norman said; "No. We support each other in our own adventures outside the job."

Eliot asked: "What was your reaction when you heard the gun go off?"

Norman said; "I called all the cops to line up against the wall to check their guns. We all thought somebody sat on their trigger or something. John was the first to be checked. The wives all lined up against the other wall so that everybody was accounted for. John didn't have his gun at all, but I searched him anyway. Michelle and John were

Seated at the front of the room."

Eliot asked: "How long did it take to search everybody's guns?"

Norman said: "Not long. Maybe 15 minutes at most. I didn't take too long with each person."

Eliot asked: "When did you find out who was the real shooter?"

Norman said: "After about 5 minutes Robert came out of the kitchen with the defendant in handcuffs."

Eliot asked: "Who called an ambulance for the victim?"

Norman said: "I think it was Robert, but I am not sure exactly. It also might have been one of the kitchen staff. You will have to ask Robert."

Eliot asked: "What was the reaction of Michelle when all this was going down?"

Normans said: "She was told to sit down in the chair and not move. She has already been trained in what to do. John trained her well."

Eliot asked: "What do you mean trained her well?"

Norman said: "All I mean is that the cops are trained to listen to me 24/7. They have never given me reason to get mad at them."

Eliot said; "No more questions your honor."

Judge O'Neil said: "Harry, you may ask your questions now."

Harry asked; "Norman, do you fraternize with your cop friends after work?"

Norman said: "My wife is friends with the wives of Robert's squad. We usually get together for holidays. The wives welcomed Michelle into their fold. They have one other person in their club. Her name is Sister Angelus. She is a nun in our parish. WE all are parishioners of the same parish. Sr. Angelus is a former teacher of ours. We all went to St. Peter's school as children."

Harry asked: "Did you graduate together?"

Norman said: "No. I was about five years older than them. Life separated us and then we came back together."

Harry asked: "Do these gathering ever turn into business meetings?"

Norman said; "No. That is against the rules. We all keep our cell phones turned on just in case something happens. Other than that business is never discussed at the dinner table. I do have the right to call meetings on the spur of the moment. The squad understand the possibility of that occurrence."

Harry asked: "How many squads do you have?"

Norman said: "We have six squads. Robert's squad is the only one I socialize with after work and on weekends."

Harry asked: "Why Robert's squad?"

Norman said: "I just told you it is the wives."

Harry said: "No more questions your honor."

Judge O'Neil said: "You may step down Norman. Eliot, call your next witness please."

Eliot said: "I request a continuance until tomorrow morning your honor."

Judge O'Neil asked: "For what reason Eliot?"

Eliot said: "I am expected in divorce court."

Judge O'Neil said: "Very well Eliot. You must not make this a habit."

Eliot said; "It won't be your honor. I promise. Thank you your honor."

Judge O'Neil said; "Apologize to the jury for this interruption on this trial."

Eliot faced the jury and said: "I apologize for this event. It won't happen again."

Judge O'Neil said: "The jury is dismissed until tomorrow morning at 9:00 a.m." Everybody left the court early with a smile on their face. They were in the elevator giggling with delight.

CHAPTER 24

Day 2 of the trial started right on time. Everybody was assembled and the judge said: "Good morning everyone. Is everybody here?"

The plaintiff said: "Yes sir. The jury is all present and accounted for. All the lawyers and defendant are present."

The judge said: "Eliot, call your first witness of the day please."

Eliot said: "I call Robert Schapiro to the stand."

Robert approached and he was sworn in as the witness."

Eliot asked: "How did you get involved with this case?"

Robert said: "I was at the wedding reception when I heard a gunshot ring out."

Eliot asked: "How did you know it was a gunshot?"

Robert said; "I am a cop. I knew there were no windows in the room, so we would not hear a car backfiring. I ran into the kitchen to see if anything happened."

Eliot asked: "What did you find?"

Robert said: "I found one chef on the floor holding his side. I looked at the wound and we all started first aid. Very basic stuff. Put pressure on the wound and such. I looked up and saw the defendant standing there with the gun in his hand. I immediately disarmed him and put the handcuffs on him. I instructed somebody to stand outside and direct the ambulance in here. Don't move the victim. Luckily he was conscious the whole time."

Eliot asked: "Did he survive?"

Robert said; "I assume so. I haven't seen or spoken to him since."

Eliot asked: "What was the victim's name?"

Robert said: "I don't remember hearing it. Maybe I never asked."

Eliot said: "No more questions your honor."

Judge O'Neil said: "Harry, do you have any questions for this witness?"

Harry asked: Have you ever had contact with the shooter before?"

Robert said: "No. I don't think I have ever seen him before."

Harry asked: "Were there any other surprises that day?"

Robert said: "Yes. We brought my dog dressed up in a wedding dress and Commissioner the Horse klopped in for John's sake. It was all in good fun. He loved it. We treat him like the son we never had."

Harry asked: "How did the defendant act when he was arrested?"

Robert said: "He was nonchalant about it. It didn't seem to bother him."

Harry asked: "Wasn't the bride related to the defendant?"

Robert said: "Yes. She is his sister."

Harry asked: "What was her reaction to seeing him?"

Robert said: "She started screaming and bellowing at him. I thought she was going to go into orbit."

Harry asked: "Was she able to talk to him alone?"

Robert said: "On Christmas Day Norman allowed him to have a visitor, but there was a cop in the room. It is standard procedure."

Harry said: "No more questions your honor."

Judge O'Neil said: "We will adjourn for the day. The lawyers and I need to have a meeting privately. Please be on time tomorrow by 9:00 a.m. Lawyers meet me in my office at 1:00 today." At 1:00 the lawyers were in the judge's office. Judge O'Neil asked: "So. How do you feel this trial is going?"

Both lawyers agreed that the trial was right on track. Eliot said: "I have the victim coming in tomorrow to testify against the defendant."

Judge O'Neil asked: "What is the name of the victim?"

Eliot said: "Ili Markham."

Judge O'Neil asked: "Does the defendant know the victim survived the shooting?"

Eliot said: "I don't think so."

Harry said: "This is news to me. I hadn't heard of that before."

Judge O'Neil said: "Both of you go home tonight and prepare your questions. Make sure they are not irrelevant to the case at hand." All parties shook hands and went home to do their homework. Judge O'Neil went home to watch the Knicks Basketball on TV. He was lucky enough not to have any homework. All he did was have a shower, light dinner, and a cup of tea.

CHAPTER 25

Day 3 of the trial started late because juror number six was late getting in. Judge O'Neil was very unhappy with this and had to waste time lecturing the jury about punctuality.

He said: "Mark McBride, I told you the first day lateness will not be tolerated. Why are you late?"

Mark said: "The bus service was kind of slow. It always has to go through the strip."

Judge O'Neil said: "Face the court and then face the jury. They all managed to follow directions. Apologize for the delay in our day." He had no choice but to do as he was told. He apologized to the court and then faced the jury and apologized again. He sat down very red faced.

Judge O'Neil said: "Now we may start our day. Eliot, call your first witness please."

Eliot said: "I call Ili Markham to the stand." As Ili approached he was sworn in as the witness. He took the stand.

Eliot asked: "How did you get involved in this case?"

Ili said: "I am the victim of this shooting."

Eliot asked: "When did this shooting take place?"

Ili said: "Christmas Eve I was working in the kitchen cooking. Somebody came up from behind me and I felt a hot sensation in my left kidney area."

Eliot asked: What were you cooking?"

Ili said: "I was cooking the mashed potatoes. We have special devices to make the potatoes into different shapes."

Eliot asked: "How long have you been working there?"

Ili said: "About a year now."

Eliot asked: "Have you had any trouble with anybody on the job?"

Ili said: "No. Everybody likes me. I do what I am told and I don't make a fuss."

Eliot asked: "How did you get this job?"

Ili said: "It was job placement from my school. I graduated top of my class."

Eliot asked: "Are you part time or full time?"

Ili said; "I am part time. I have another job full time. My employer is aware of this job. He lets me take off whenever necessary."

Eliot asked: "Do you make trouble for the other employees?"

Ili said: "No. I don't. I just do my job as best I can."

Eliot asked: "Do you talk much to the other employees?"

Ili said; "No. I just concentrate on what I am doing. I tune everyone else out."

Eliot said: "No more questions your honor."

Judge O'Neil said: "Harry, do you have any questions for this witness?"

Harry said: "Yes your honor. Now Ili, please tell us how it was that you were shot?"

Ili said: "I felt a hot sensation in my left kidney."

Harry asked: "What happened when you got to the hospital?"

Ili said: "I took off my shirt and they took X-rays. That is when they found the bullet in me."

Harry asked: "Did they remove it?"

Ili said; "Yes they did."

Harry asked: "What hospital did you go to?"

Ili said: "I went to Las Vegas General."

Harry asked: "Did you suffer any kidney damage as a result of this shooting?"

Ili said: "I won't know until sometime in the future. In the meantime I have to take regular urine tests to see if any problems have come up. The blood tests don't bother me, but I don't think I will ever get used to peeing in a cup."

Harry asked: "Are you fully recovered?"

Ili said: "I am recovered enough to work. I have to wash my hands all the time anyway working with food. I am very meticulous about cross contamination and all that."

Harry asked: "Have you ever met the defendant before?"

Ili said: "No. I think this is the first time I set eyes on him. He doesn't look familiar at all."

Harry said: "No more questions your honor."

Judge O'Neil said: "You may step down Ili. Eliot, call your next witness please."

Eliot said: "I call Michelle to the stand." As Michelle approached the stand she was sworn in as the witness.

Michelle looked a little nervous about testifying against her brother.

Judge O'Neil said: "Relax Michelle. Just answer the questions as best you can. You have nothing to worry about."

Eliot asked: "What is your relationship with the defendant?"

Michelle said: "He is my brother."

Eliot asked; "When was the last time you saw him?"

Michelle said: "He left home in 1998. He called a few times to let us know he is in New York. He is safe. He said he had a regular job."

Eliot asked; "A regular job doing what?"

Michelle said: "He said he was a messenger. He called on Sept. 10, 2001 and told us he was fine. Then Sept. 11th happened and we never heard from him again. We just assumed that he was caught up in the melee. He never called again."

Eliot asked: "What drove him to New York from Colorado?"

Michelle said: "As parents often do they want the kids to stay where they are and take care of them. My father said he loved him just enough to let him go. They weren't going anywhere."

Eliot asked: "Were your parents upset that he never called?"

Michelle said: "It killed my father. As each day passed my mother got more and more upset. She just withdrew totally. It was the emotional hurt of Sept. 11th that killed her. She died six months after dad died."

Eliot asked: "How long has he been living in Las Vegas?"

Michelle said; "I don't know. He was the last person I expected to see. He just appeared without warning out of the blue."

Eliot asked: "Do you work?"

Michelle said: "Yes. I am a sales clerk."

Eliot asked: "Are you missing work today for this trial?"

Michelle said: "Yes. But I can go in for half a day. My boss likes me and I have already proven myself worthy of working there. I promised him it wouldn't be a habit not to come in."

Eliot said: "No more questions for this witness."

Judge O'Neil said: "Harry, do you have any questions for this witness?"

Harry said: "Yes your honor. Michelle, were you able to talk to your brother in the jail?"

Michelle said: "Yes. But not alone. We had no privacy. There was Norman and a uniformed cop in the room with us. I had to stand in the middle of the room and not approach the bars. The uniformed cop had to search me to make sure I don't have a key to the cell. I just let him do it. I knew he only had a job to do. I had to empty my pockets and leave everything on the table. Norman explained the procedure."

Harry asked; "Were there any other prisoners?"

Michelle said: "No sir. My brother was the only one."

Harry asked; "Would John your husband know about that?"

Michelle said: "No. He has been on vacation for about two weeks now."

Harry asked: "When does he go back to work?"

Michelle said: "He went back yesterday, but he is a detective, so he has nothing to do with the prisoners. His job is unrelated to prisoners in jail."

Harry said: "No more questions your honor."

Judge O'Neil said: You may step down Michelle. Ladies and gentlemen of the jury. Because of the late hour we will adjourn until tomorrow morning. Have a good night everyone." With that everybody rose and left the courthouse.

CHAPTER 26

ay 4 of the trial started right on time. Judge O'Neil said: "Good morning ladies and gentlemen. Thank you for obeying my orders to be on time. Eliot, call your first witness please."

Eliot said: "I call Donald McCormack to the stand."

Donald approached the stand and was sworn in by the bailiff.

Eliot asked: "Donald, when did you leave home?"

Donald said: "I let home when I was eighteen years old."

Eliot asked: "Where was home until then?"

Donald said: "Home was Denver, Colorado."

Eliot asked: "Why did you leave home?"

Donald said: "I had a fight with my father. He told me to go out and live on my own, so I did. I never looked back. I admit to calling my mother every now and then just to keep her informed that I am still alive."

Eliot asked: "Did you get counseling for your fighting?"

Donald said: "No. I was just being a teenage brat."

Eliot asked: "Where did you go when you left home?"

Donald said: "I walked to New York. I simply walked in an easterly direction. I had no money, so I had to pick up loose change along the street. That is why I didn't hitchhike along the highway. People don't usually drop change out of their cars."

Eliot asked: "Were you ever arrested?"

Donald said: "Yes. That was heavenly because I got a shower and 3 square meals a day."

Eliot asked: "What were you arrested for?"

Donald said: "Shoplifting. That happened in Ohio. It was a Walmart store."

Eliot asked: "How long were you in jail?"

Donald said: "About three days."

Eliot asked: "Why didn't you join the military?"

Donald said: "No. I am too sensitive to people screaming in my face. The military was never an option."

Eliot asked: "How did you get along with Michelle?"

Donald said: "I didn't. We were never close. I did torture her most of her life."

Eliot asked: "Why did you shoot Ili?"

Donald said: "I remember him from New York. He owed me money and he skipped town."

Eliot asked; "How long have you been in Las Vegas?"

Donald said; "I have been here for maybe six months now."

Eliot asked: "How did you get here?"

Donald said: "I walked. Again it was the city streets."

Eliot asked: "When did you catch up to the victim Ili?"

Donald said: "My second day in town. I just followed him around and learned his schedule."

Eliot asked: "Where have you been staying all this time?"

Donald said: "I have been staying underground. Miraculously they have showerheads down there."

Eliot asked: "Where are your clothes?"

Donald said: "I leave them underground. Whatever is still there it was meant for me to have."

Eliot asked: "Where did you get the gun to shoot Ili?"

Donald said: "I found it underground. There are a lot of things buried down there. People think the cops don't want to search down there with all the rats."

Eliot said: "No more questions your honor."

Judge O'Neil said: "Harry, do you have any questions for this witness?"

Harry said: "No questions for this witness. Eliot stole my notes and covered all the bases for me."

Judge O'Neil said; "We will now break for lunch. After lunch we will resume here for closing arguments. Lawyers, my chambers immediately." The judge admonished them severely and screamed out: 'What did I tell you about acting like a child in my courtroom? That was totally inappropriate. Eliot, did you really steal his notes?"

Eliot said: "No sir. I never looked at them."

Judge O'Neil asked: "Why did you just say that in my courtroom?"

Harry said: "For drama sir. I didn't intend any disrespect to the court."

Judge O'Neil said; "Don't let it happen again."

Harry said: "It won't sir. I promise."

Judge O'Neil said: "Go get something to eat."

CHAPTER 27

After lunch everybody returned to the courtroom just as instructed. Judge O'Neil said: "Eliot, you may begin your closing arguments when ready."

Eliot got up and said: "Thank you your honor. Ladies and gentlemen. It is no secret that the defendant shot an innocent person. Luckily he survived. In today's economy you would do anything to get money. My client chose not to join society and just wander the earth sucking up the oxygen. There are better ways of handling a situation like this. He could have talked to the guy. But no. He decided to shoot first and ask questions later. This is not the OK Corral. This is real life here. There are no excuses for the almost taking of a life. He chose not to be a productive member of society. He thought he could take the easy way out and live off the grid. Life has a way of catching up with you. Thank you."

CHAPTER 28

Judge O'Neil said: "Harry, you may begin your closing arguments when ready."

Harry said: "Thank you your honor. Ladies and gentlemen of the jury. It is no secret that my client shot at somebody. He did not actually kill him though. In a lot of ways my client is still acting like an immature teenager. He doesn't know how to deal with people. He didn't want him to die, he was just sending him a message not to owe people money. You must find my client not guilty of attempted murder. If anything you should send my client to a psychiatric hospital, not a jail cell. Thank you."

Judge O'Neil said; "Ladies and gentlemen of the jury. You have now heard both sides of the story. Your job is to select a head foreman and decide if he is guilty of attempted murder. Your names are all kept secret. I promise nobody will ever call you afterwards. You will send a note to the bailiff.

Bailiff, please escort these people into the jury room. Meantime lawyers will meet in my chambers immediately." The lawyers did as they were told. When they sat down it was just small talk. It was a waiting game to get to a verdict. They both thought they were going to be the winner in this case. The judge reminded them that there were no winners when a man's life has been permanently altered.

Meanwhile back in the jury room juror number six volunteered to be the jury spokesperson. Nobody objected. Nobody really wanted that job anyway. After about a half hour of drinking coffee and chattering they got down to business. It took only one vote to find him guilty. The bailiff sent a not to the judge.

CHAPTER 29

When they reassembled in the courtroom juror number six passed the note to the judge. He said; "Will the defendant please rise." The defendant rose and the judge said; "What is your verdict?"

Juror number six said: "We find the defendant guilty of attempted murder."

The judge asked; "So say you all?"

Juror number six said; "Yes sir. So say us all."

The judge said: "Ladies an gentlemen of the jury. Thank you for your service. You are excused. Please return to the jury assembly room for dismissal."

When the jury left the room the judge said: "Defendant Donald, please stand up for sentencing. I find you to do one year in a mental hospital and five years probation. Bailiff, remove this defendant down to the tombs and await transportation to the city mental hospital.

THE END

Here is a synopsis of my next novel coming soon.

The kidnapping of Sr. Angelus

One week before Halloween Sr. Angelus was kidnapped in front of the whole school. The children didn't know if it was trick or treat trick or if it was real. The Mother Superior of the order was present and she sprang into action. She called the squad and Robert's team was assembled within the hour. They first had to toss around ideas like if it was Al Qaida or angry parents or who was behind it. They eliminated the Al Qaida idea. Mother Superior took over the duties until Sr. Angelus was returned safe and sound. She called the pastor Father Raaser and informed him of the development. How will they solve this mystery and where is she hiding? They had to go on National TV for help. They got tips from all over the world. She was in California, Florida, Australia, and even Ireland. The kidnappers would be calling for ransome. For some reason that call never came in. Buy the book and see who is behind the mystery and which member of the team is responsible for finding her.

Blessing to you all for all my faithful readers.